# OLIVER

B

PIONEER VALLEY EDUCATIONAL PRESS, INC.

"Look at the ball, Oliver," said Evan. "Go get it!"

The ball went up, up, up.
The ball went
down, down, down.

3

"Oliver, go get the ball," said Evan.

Oliver looked at the ball. "Meow," he said.

Evan went and got
the ball.
"Look at the ball, Oliver!"

The ball went up, up, up.

The ball went
down,
down,
down.

"Come on, Oliver,"
said Evan.
"Go get the ball."

Oliver sat and looked
at the ball.
"Meow," he said.

"Oh, no," said Mom.
The ball of yarn went
down,
down,
down.

"Meow!" said Oliver.